AMAZING

PLANETS

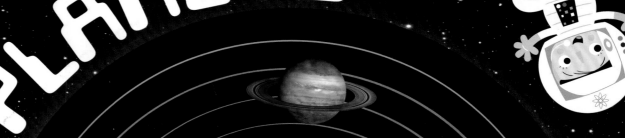

make
believe
ideas

WHAT IS A PLANET?

A planet is a huge, natural object that travels around, or **orbits**, a **star**. Our **universe** is filled with trillions of planets **orbiting** their own **stars**.

orbit

Planets are OUT OF THIS WORLD!

planet

OUR MILKY WAY **GALAXY** HAS A PLANET ABOUT 13 BILLION YEARS OLD.

 THE SURFACE OF ONE PLANET IN OUR **GALAXY** IS ALMOST AS HOT AS THE SUN.

 SCIENTISTS HAVE FOUND PLANETS COVERED IN GAS, ICE, WATER, LAVA, AND EVEN DIAMONDS!

DID YOU KNOW?

Some planets aren't perfectly round. They bulge in the middle because they're spinning so fast.

bulge

star

The SOLAR SYSTEM

Our solar system is a group of eight planets **orbiting** a **star** we call the Sun. It also has more than 200 **moons** and millions of small rocky objects.

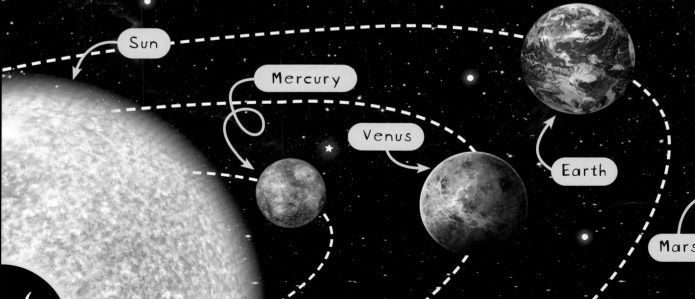

Sun

Mercury

Venus

Earth

Mars

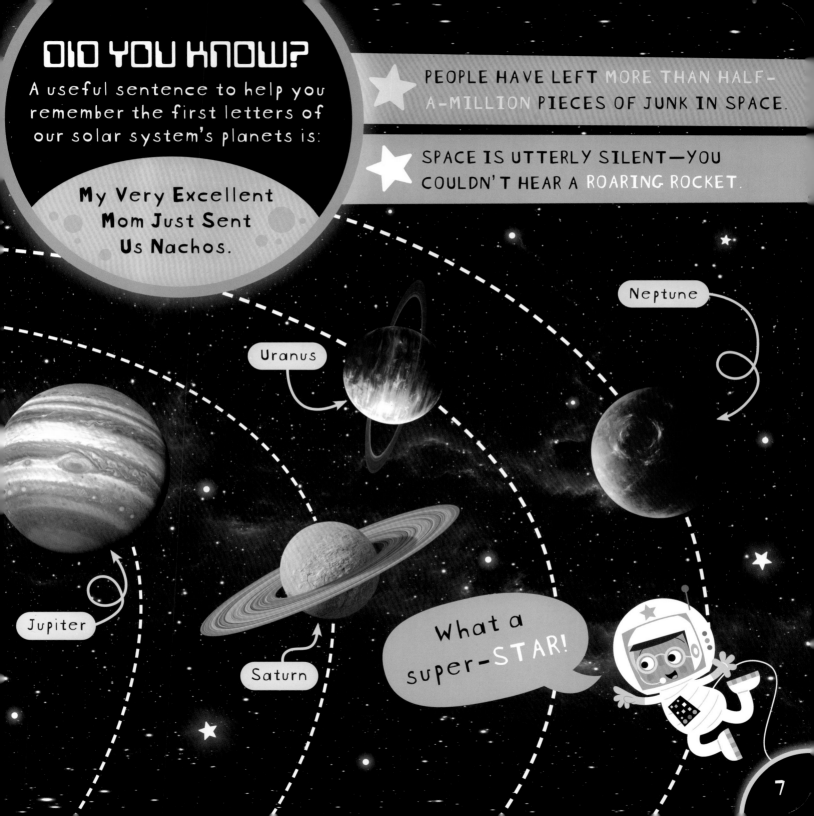

OIO YOU KNOW?

A useful sentence to help you remember the first letters of our solar system's planets is:

My Very Excellent Mom Just Sent Us Nachos.

PEOPLE HAVE LEFT MORE THAN HALF-A-MILLION PIECES OF JUNK IN SPACE.

SPACE IS UTTERLY SILENT—YOU COULDN'T HEAR A ROARING ROCKET.

Neptune

Uranus

Jupiter

Saturn

What a super-STAR!

ROCKY PLANETS

Planets with rocky surfaces are called **terrestrial** planets. Mercury, Venus, Earth, and Mars are the solar system's four **terrestrial** planets.

volcanic mountain

surface of Venus

a canyon on Earth

MERCURY HAS WRINKLES FROM RIDGES AND CRACKS ALL OVER ITS ROCKY SURFACE.

 SOME SCIENTISTS THINK VENUS WAS SMOTHERED BY A GIANT LAVA FLOOD MILLIONS OF YEARS AGO.

 HUGE DUST STORMS CAN LAST FOR MONTHS ON MARS.

EVERY DAY, EARTH IS SPRINKLED WITH COSMIC DUST FROM VAPORIZED COMETS.

DID YOU KNOW?

Terrestrial planets often have mountains, craters, canyons, and volcanoes on their surfaces.

volcano on Venus

craters on Mercury

These planets ROCK!

a volcano on Mars

MERCURY

The closest planet to our Sun is Mercury. It's only slightly bigger than Earth's **moon**, making it the smallest planet in our solar system.

Luckily, I brought my SUNGLASSES!

Sun

a huge crater with smaller craters inside

YOU COULD JUMP THREE TIMES HIGHER ON MERCURY THAN ON EARTH.

THERE'S A CRATER ON MERCURY THAT'S TWICE AS WIDE AS LOS ANGELES.

BY DAY, MERCURY IS SEVEN TIMES HOTTER THAN THE SAHARA DESERT.

MERCURY HAS NO MOONS BECAUSE THE SUN'S STRONGER GRAVITY STEALS THEM.

HOW BIG?

Earth   Mercury

FACT FILE

AVERAGE DISTANCE FROM SUN:
36 MILLION MILES (58 MILLION KM)

CAR DRIVE FROM EARTH: 93 YEARS

1 DAY LASTS: 59 EARTH DAYS

1 YEAR LASTS: 88 EARTH DAYS

PLANET TYPE: TERRESTRIAL

NUMBER OF MOONS: 0

VENUS

The hottest planet in our solar system is Venus. Its thick **atmosphere** traps the Sun's heat, making its surface hotter than a pizza oven.

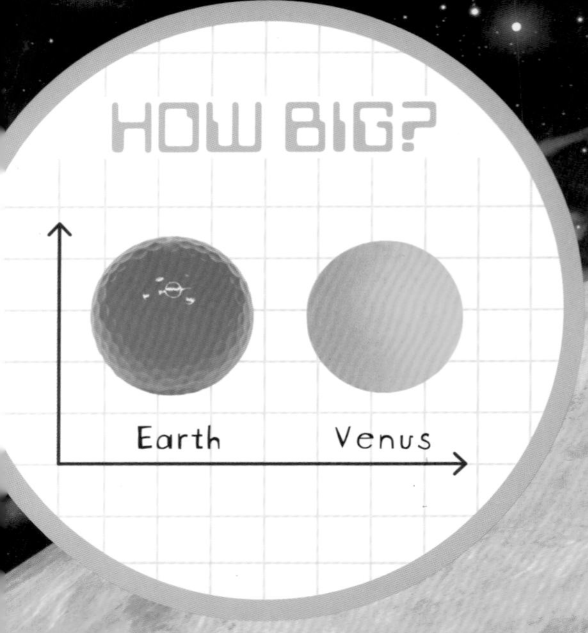

smelly clouds

HOW BIG?

Earth   Venus

This planet needs a
METEOR SHOWER!

SOME SCIENTISTS THINK VENUS MAY HAVE UP TO ONE MILLION VOLCANOES.

 A DAY ON VENUS IS LONGER THAN ONE OF ITS YEARS.

 THE RAIN ON VENUS IS MADE OF SKIN-BURNING SULFURIC ACID.

VENUS IS COVERED IN YELLOW CLOUDS THAT SMELL LIKE ROTTEN EGGS.

DID YOU KNOW?

Venus was the first planet to be explored by spacecraft. NASA's Mariner 2 flew by and scanned its surface in 1962.

FACT FILE

AVERAGE DISTANCE FROM SUN:
67 MILLION MILES (108 MILLION KM)

CAR DRIVE FROM EARTH: 42 YEARS

1 DAY LASTS: 243 EARTH DAYS

1 YEAR LASTS: 225 EARTH DAYS

PLANET TYPE: TERRESTRIAL

NUMBER OF MOONS: 0

EARTH

Earth is the only known planet with living things. It has the right **atmosphere** and the right temperature for life. About eight billion people live here.

I can see my HOUSE from here!

DID YOU KNOW?

About 300 million years ago, Earth had just one big area of land, surrounded by ocean.

EARTH'S LAYERS

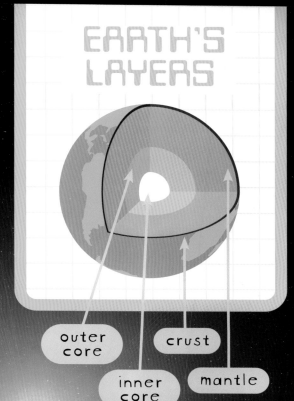

outer core

crust

inner core

mantle

 EARTH'S INNER CORE IS ABOUT AS HOT AS THE SURFACE OF THE SUN.

 EARTH IS STRUCK BY LIGHTNING ABOUT 44 TIMES EVERY SECOND.

EARTH HAS NEARLY NINE MILLION DIFFERENT PLANT AND ANIMAL SPECIES.

 EARTH'S SURFACE HAS THREE TIMES AS MUCH WATER AS DRY LAND.

FACT FILE

AVERAGE DISTANCE FROM SUN:
93 MILLION MILES (150 MILLION KM)

CAR DRIVE TO SUN: 152 YEARS

1 DAY LASTS: 24 HOURS

1 YEAR LASTS: 365 EARTH DAYS

PLANET TYPE: TERRESTRIAL

NUMBER OF MOONS: 1

15

MARS

The second smallest planet in our solar system is Mars. Its red color comes from lots of rusty iron in its rocks and soil.

solar-powered scouting helicopter

laser camera

NASA'S MARS ROVER, PERSEVERANCE

That looks WHEELY cool!

14-year power supply

underground radar

HOW BIG?

Earth   Mars

rock and soil analyzer

rock drill

Olympus Mons

Everest

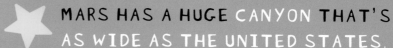

★ MARS HAS A **HUGE** CANYON **THAT'S AS WIDE AS THE UNITED STATES.**

★ MARS ONCE HAD FLOWING WATER AND MAY HAVE BEEN HOME TO LIVING THINGS.

★ FINE DUST IN THE SKY MAKES SUNSETS ON MARS LOOK BLUE.

★ MARS HAS A VOLCANO **THREE TIMES THE HEIGHT** OF MOUNT EVEREST.

FACT FILE

AVERAGE DISTANCE FROM SUN:
142 MILLION MILES (228 MILLION KM)

CAR DRIVE FROM EARTH: 79 YEARS

1 DAY LASTS: 24 HOURS, 37 MINUTES

1 YEAR LASTS: 687 EARTH DAYS

PLANET TYPE: TERRESTRIAL

NUMBER OF MOONS: 2

17

GAS GIANTS

Gas giants are huge planets made mainly of gases and liquids. In their center, there may be a hard, rocky core. Jupiter and Saturn are our solar system's two gas giants.

Jupiter

swirling clouds of water and ammonia

JUPITER'S LAYERS

liquid hydrogen

rocky core

hydrogen and helium gases

 GAS GIANTS OFTEN HAVE LOTS OF MOONS—JUPITER HAS 80.

 BEYOND OUR SOLAR SYSTEM, THERE ARE BIG GAS GIANTS CALLED SUPER-JUPITERS.

 ON GAS GIANTS, THE ATMOSPHERE AND SURFACE BLEND TOGETHER.

BETWEEN MARS AND JUPITER IS THE FROST LINE. GAS GIANTS CAN ONLY SURVIVE PAST THIS LINE.

That's fan-GAS-tic!

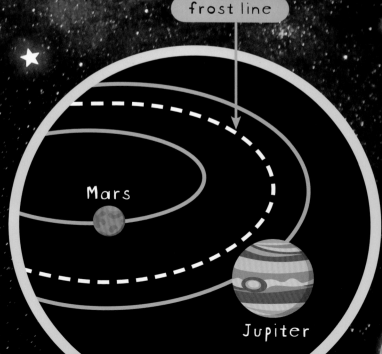

frost line

Mars

Jupiter

JUPITER

The biggest planet in our solar system is Jupiter. It's more than twice the size of all the solar system's other planets put together.

No wonder it's called a gas GIANT!

HOW BIG?

Earth   Jupiter

huge storm

 JUPITER'S GREAT RED SPOT IS A STORM LARGER THAN EARTH.

 JUPITER'S **GRAVITY** PULLS IN **ASTEROIDS** THAT MIGHT OTHERWISE HIT EARTH.

JUPITER IS SO BIG THAT ABOUT 1,300 EARTHS COULD FIT INSIDE IT.

 ONE OF JUPITER'S **MOONS** HAS A MASSIVE UNDERGROUND OCEAN.

FACT FILE

AVERAGE DISTANCE FROM SUN:
484 MILLION MILES (778 MILLION KM)

CAR DRIVE FROM EARTH: 637 YEARS

1 DAY LASTS: 9 HOURS, 56 MINUTES

1 YEAR LASTS: 4,333 EARTH DAYS

PLANET TYPE: GAS GIANT

NUMBER OF MOONS: 80

SATURN

The farthest planet that most people can see without a telescope is Saturn. Its striped rings are made from billions of chunks of ice and rock.

Now that's inspi-RING!

Saturn's rings

SCIENTISTS THINK SATURN'S LARGEST **MOON** MAY HAVE TINY CREATURES LIVING ON IT.

IF YOU PUT SATURN IN A GIANT SWIMMING POOL, IT WOULD FLOAT.

SOME ICE AND ROCKS IN SATURN'S RINGS ARE AS BIG AS EARTH'S MOUNTAINS.

LIGHTNING STRIKES ON SATURN ARE 1,000 TIMES MORE POWERFUL THAN ON EARTH.

HOW BIG?

Earth   Saturn

FACT FILE

AVERAGE DISTANCE FROM SUN: 886 MILLION MILES (1.4 BILLION KM)

CAR DRIVE FROM EARTH: 1,292 YEARS

1 DAY LASTS: 10 HOURS, 34 MINUTES

1 YEAR LASTS: 10,756 EARTH DAYS

PLANET TYPE: GAS GIANT

NUMBER OF MOONS: ≥ 63

ICE GIANTS

Ice giants have a thinner gas layer than gas giants. Below that, they have a thick layer of chemicals such as water and ammonia in a slushy, or icy, state. Uranus and Neptune are our solar system's two ice giants.

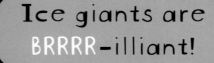

Ice giants are BRRRR-illiant!

Uranus

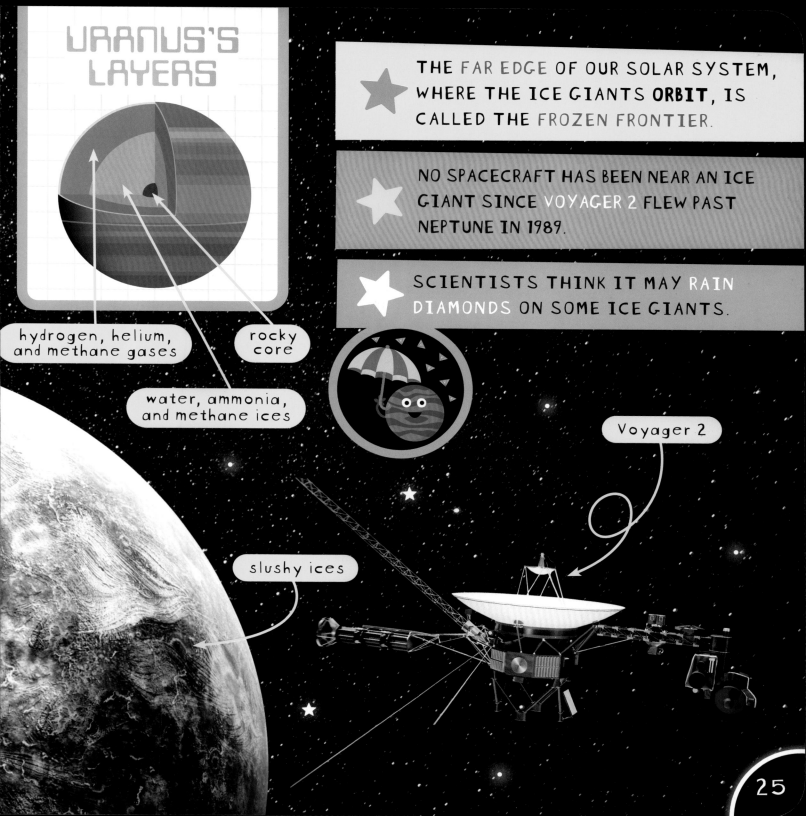

URANUS'S LAYERS

hydrogen, helium, and methane gases

rocky core

water, ammonia, and methane ices

slushy ices

THE FAR EDGE OF OUR SOLAR SYSTEM, WHERE THE ICE GIANTS **ORBIT**, IS CALLED **THE** FROZEN FRONTIER.

NO SPACECRAFT HAS BEEN NEAR AN ICE GIANT SINCE VOYAGER 2 FLEW PAST NEPTUNE IN 1989.

SCIENTISTS THINK IT MAY RAIN DIAMONDS ON SOME ICE GIANTS.

Voyager 2

URANUS

The only planet in our solar system that **rotates** on its side is Uranus. It looks blue because of the methane gas in its **atmosphere**.

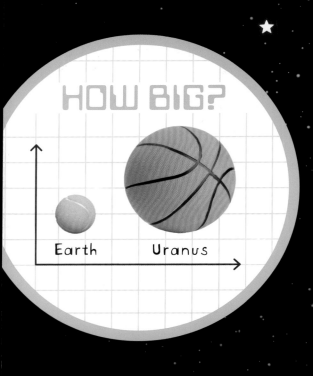

HOW BIG?

Earth   Uranus

FACT FILE

AVERAGE DISTANCE FROM SUN:
1.8 BILLION MILES (2.9 BILLION KM)

CAR DRIVE FROM EARTH: 2,760 YEARS

1 DAY LASTS: 17 HOURS, 14 MINUTES

1 YEAR LASTS: 30,687 EARTH DAYS

PLANET TYPE: ICE GIANT

NUMBER OF MOONS: 27

TEMPERATURES ON URANUS CAN BE MORE THAN TWICE AS COLD AS ANTARCTICA.

ONE OF URANUS'S **MOONS** HAS A CLIFF THAT'S 50 TIMES TALLER THAN THE EMPIRE STATE BUILDING.

WITH PERFECT EYESIGHT, YOU CAN SEE URANUS WITHOUT A TELESCOPE.

URANUS'S SIDEWAYS **ROTATION** MAY HAVE BEEN CAUSED WHEN AN **ASTEROID** HIT IT.

Uranus? More like Uran-ICE!

fast-moving winds, or jet stream

27

NEPTUNE

The solar system's farthest planet from the Sun is Neptune. It's more than 30 times as far from the Sun as Earth.

giant storm with **supersonic** winds

HOW BIG?

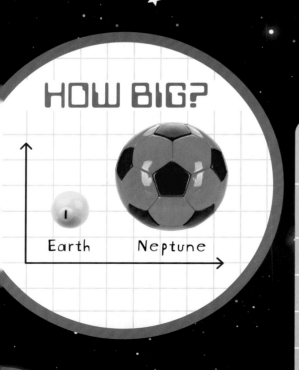

Earth   Neptune

FACT FILE

AVERAGE DISTANCE FROM SUN:
2.8 BILLION MILES (4.5 BILLION KM)

CAR DRIVE FROM EARTH: 4,410 YEARS

1 DAY LASTS: 16 HOURS

1 YEAR LASTS: 60,190 EARTH DAYS

PLANET TYPE: ICE GIANT

NUMBER OF MOONS: 14

This planet **BLOWS ME AWAY!**

Neptune has five rings, but they are hard to see because they are made from dust and dark rocks.

one of Neptune's moons

 IN ABOUT 3.6 BILLION YEARS, NEPTUNE WILL COLLIDE WITH ITS LARGEST **MOON**.

 THE MIDDLE OF THE DAY ON NEPTUNE IS ONLY AS BRIGHT AS DUSK ON EARTH.

 NEPTUNE HAS MOVING DARK SPOTS THAT ARE GIANT STORMS, LASTING UP TO FIVE YEARS.

 WIND SPEEDS ON NEPTUNE CAN BE AS FAST AS A **SUPERSONIC** JET.

DWARF PLANETS

Dwarf planets are rounded like other planets, but much smaller. Also they have other objects in their **orbit** pathways. This is because they aren't large enough to pull those objects into them or to push them away, as full-size planets do.

Pluto

nitrogen ice plain

crater

THE DWARF PLANET HAUMEA'S FAST SPIN HAS FORCED IT INTO AN EGG SHAPE.

EACH KNOWN DWARF PLANET IN OUR SOLAR SYSTEM IS SMALLER THAN EARTH'S MOON.

CERES HAS BRIGHT SPOTS ON ITS SURFACE THAT MAY BE ICE OR SALT.

They don't look that SMALL to me!

PLUTO WAS CALLED A PLANET FOR 76 YEARS BEFORE IT WAS RENAMED A DWARF PLANET IN 2006.

The Solar System's Known Dwarf Planets

| Ceres | Pluto | Haumea | Makemake | Eris |

EXOPLANETS

An exoplanet is a planet outside our solar system. More than 5,000 exoplanets have been found so far. One, called Kepler 186f, could be the right size and distance from its **star** to support life.

Kepler 186f

How EXO-ting!

GLOSSARY

asteroid a rocky object smaller than a dwarf planet that orbits the Sun

atmosphere a layer of gas around a planet. It is often a mix of a few different gases.

galaxy a massive collection of stars, planets, and other matter. Our solar system is in the Milky Way galaxy.

gravity the invisible force that pulls a smaller object toward a larger object. The larger an object, the more gravity it has.

moon a natural object that orbits a planet, dwarf planet, or other large object, such as an asteroid

orbit the path an object takes around a star or planet. Orbits are often oval shaped.

rotate to spin around. The time a planet takes to rotate once on its axis equals one day.

star a giant, glowing ball of hot, burning gas. Earth's closest star is the Sun.

supersonic faster than the speed of sound

terrestrial a planet made mainly of rocks or metals with a hard surface

universe everything that exists, including stars, planets, and billions of galaxies